A Different Little Doggy

written by **Heather Whittaker**

illustrated by **Scott Alberts**

Pen-Tech Professional LLC

First Edition
ISBN 13: 978-0-9820962-2-2

Published by Pen-Tech Professional
PO Box 67
Greenville, WI 54942

www.adifferentlittledoggy.com

For Mary and my girls...
I'm very happy that we
are different.

Hello, my name is Taz.

I'm a different little doggy...

...a different little doggy,
unlike all others.

Some call me little.
I am very, very small.

But, I like it that way.
I wouldn't want to be tall.

Because I am small,

I find all kinds of fun places.

And when playing
with friends,

I can still win all the races.

We went to the doctor, and he did an x-ray to see
what exactly had happened to me.

The doctor fixed me right up.
I now have pins in my knees.

I can do so many new things now
with skill and with ease.

I can stand
on my toes...

...and can sit
like a froggy.

I am just such a
different little doggy.

I look different than others.
Their ears stand up straight.

My ears are floppy but
that's a wonderful trait!

My ears make me look oh so cute and so cuddly.

No matter how old, I still look like a puppy!

Different dogs come in many different colors...

I am black, tan, and white which is different than some others.

I have friends that are
gray, brown, red, and white.
And, when playing together,
we wag our tails in delight!

There is just one more way
that I'm also a bit different.

You see, I lost my sight in a
blink... in an instant.

When I woke up one day,
I found I could no longer see,
but it really does not matter
because I am still me.

I learned to get around, so I can still run and play.
I just do it in a bit different way.

I now see with my nose
and feel with my toes.

It's how I get around
even when it snows.

As you can see,
being different is OK.
There is a reason
God made me this way.

So next time you meet
someone different than you,
walk right up and say
"How do you do?

I like to dance,
skip, jump and run.
Would you like to play?
It's sure to be FUN!"

The

End

Meet the creative team...

Heather Whittaker is a Wisconsin based business & motivational speaker and author of several books that incorporate stories from the lives of her dogs Tinker, Taz, Erin, Sadie, and Roxie together with her own experiences to motivate others. This one being her favorite, "A Different Little Doggy", teaches children the importance of embracing their own differences and accepting the differences of others. Connect with Heather and learn more about her canine friends at www.heatherwhittaker.com.

Scott Alberts loves to bring characters to life through illustration. His unique talents spring from a deep understanding of graphic design and fine arts necessary for fantastic realism in the publishing arena. Based in Appleton, Wisconsin, Scott has gained national recognition as an expert in illustrative arts. He enjoys creating large scale murals and background set pieces that accompany on-stage productions, and working with authors to develop authentic, endearing characters. Learn more about him at www.scottalberts.com.